DIRTY HITMEN

Steamy BWWM Mafia

Leandra Camilli

CONTENTS

CHAPTER 1

"**A**re you going to tell me more about you?" He asked, his voice sounding like music to my ears. There was just something different about it, and I couldn't put my finger on it. Perhaps it was his accent. It was different. I wasn't used to it and it showed. I wanted to see him in front of me, but he was probably miles away.

I was saying that because it was the first time that we were calling. Before, we chatted online. On the Facebook group, where we didn't have to do more than write on our keyboards. He was quite welcoming, doing everything I wanted, including sending me some dick pics, something I was missing already.

"Maybe I should, but I don't know if I will," I responded and he groaned. I could tell that he didn't like it, but there was nothing he could do about it. After all, if there was something I liked doing, it was teasing, and he was falling right into my trap.

I was in my apartment, turning off the faucet. I looked out the window, checking out the cars driving down the road. It was serene. I couldn't even see many people perambulating in the streets, something a little odd and yet, also common and mundane.

"You are always such a tease," he grumbled, and, for a moment, I thought he was going to hang up on me. But when the seconds passed and that didn't happen, I knew I had him wrapped around my finger. So much so that I was already smiling.

"Can you do something for me? It's been a while," I said and I wondered if he was going to do it. It would be a shame if he didn't, but then again, he was always a box full of surprises.

"What do you want me to do for you?" He asked and his voice was much lower than before, and also much sexier. I could almost feel him in front of me, remembering that he was nothing more than someone imaginary. I mean, I knew he existed, but it was different knowing that and knowing what he looked like, and he wasn't too keen on showing up here.

And yet, I was also a little reluctant about inviting him to my place. Something about it was telling me that I shouldn't, that he was dangerous, even though I didn't even know him. Other than talking to him over the phone, I didn't really know much about the guy.

Outside, it was dark and the only thing illuminating the street in front of the apartment was the light bulb hanging from the street pole. It wasn't ugly, but it wasn't inviting, either. Why? It was pretty simple. Even though the light was bright, it wasn't bright enough to keep the shadows away, and I could see plenty of dangerous criminals lurking in them.

And one other thing that would keep me awake at night, even though it didn't, was the fact that even the guy that was calling me could be outside, watching me from afar. He would be in the shadows, talking to me, watching everything I did, and yet, something about that turned me on. It made me feel sexy, even wanted, even though I knew it wasn't right. I knew the dangers of those thoughts, which was one reason why I wasn't even thinking about them right now.

"Spit it out already. You're making me think that you are probably not worth it," he grumbled and I lied down on my bed. I wanted to masturbate, but without something extra to make me feel more excited, I couldn't. And the fact was that this moment was excellent for that. The room was quiet and so were my neighbors. Sometimes I could hear them making love right above my room, but not this time, which was refreshing.

"Can you send me one of those pics?" I asked, holding my breath. My hand was already going down and I was picturing myself seeing his dick pic on my phone, all of his 10 inches asking me to worship them, and asking myself when I would finally muster enough courage to ask him to come. Why? It was pretty simple. I was a virgin and I wanted to have my first time, even though I knew that with someone so much more experienced, I would probably be left at a disadvantage.

And yet, something about him told me that he would probably be careful and loving with me.

"You want one of *those* pics?" He asked, almost making him look like he didn't know what I was talking about, even though he knew. He knew it well because this was far from the first time that I was requesting that.

I nodded, biting my bottom lip. I closed my eyes and pictured that he was right in front of me, above me, with his arms on either side of me, and cornering me against the bed. I could already imagine his lips coming in contact with mine, his tongue sneaking past my lips, and then his hands working my skin, massaging it, making me feel things I never even thought possible.

It would be the most amazing, most thrilling thing that ever happened in my life, and he was aware of it. So much so that I wasn't surprised when he chuckled, the sound of him lowering his zipper coming through the call.

"I think I can do a lot more than that," he announced and his voice was even sexier than before, something I didn't think was possible.

"I'm waiting for it," I said and then I reopened my eyes when my phone buzzed slightly, even against my ear. I knew it was going to happen, but my heart was still speeding up when it did.

My finger was hovering over the screen of the phone and I almost didn't want to press the notification icon. It knew that it would make me feel things I shouldn't, and yet I was aware that there was no coming back. Not from this. After all, I didn't want to disappoint Karp. The mysterious Russian that could make me feel so many things, and most of them could make me drool so much…

And yet, I still pressed my finger to the notification, loading up his photo, and it was as exciting as I thought. My clit was already hard and giving me a sensation of prickling, something that wasn't common. Or it was common when we were sexting, and now was one of those times.

His cock was nothing short of jaw-dropping, making me check it out carefully, from bottom to top, and scrutinize all the details. If there was something I wanted to do with it right now, it was wrapping my fingers around it, feeling how massive and heavy it was. And it wouldn't be just that, but also how potent he was, especially in terms of making me feel as though I was on the moon.

I could just imagine his balls slapping against my butt, over and over again, and then he would pop my hymen, and I would finally be able to tell all my bitch friends that I wasn't a virgin anymore. And they would look at me with envy in their eyes, wondering how I had sex with a seductive, tall, and imposing Russian that could even make their boyfriends and husbands look like nothing more than puny, insignificant simps.

I started to rub my clit with my finger slowly before picking up the speed. Playing with my pussy folds, it was even more heart-tightening than I thought possible. I could imagine him then coming inside of me and even though it shouldn't happen, I could also picture having his baby.

My cunt was soaking wet, my clit was throbbing, and my back arched. I could feel my orgasm coming and when it exploded, it would also wash over my body, fading every shred of stress and anxiety locked in me.

I would think that nothing was better than that, only to realize that it wasn't even the tip of that iceberg. And even though I knew he wasn't the romantic type, I knew that he would hug me from behind and then he would fall asleep with his arms wrapped around me.

Following that, my body started to convulse when I couldn't hold it back anymore. I finally came and it was everything I thought it was going to be. My body was so hot I could feel the sweat coming out of the pores and making it feel messy and slick. I gripped the bedsheets, but it wasn't like it was going to help me with anything.

I bit my bottom lip so hard that I drew out blood, and that wasn't even the beginning of it. Or maybe I should be saying that it was already the end of it.

I was already returning to my usual, boring self, and so was my life. I had the most amazing, explosive orgasm of my life, but it was still not enough. When I reopened my eyes and found out that I was still in my old, moldy room, I couldn't help but wonder when I would finally grow a backbone and leave this place.

Why? It was pretty simple. I had the money for that, but I didn't want to spend it. I wanted to save up, to start building my wealth, but I couldn't do that if I was living in a more expensive, luxurious place.

And then, my phone buzzed again. It wasn't Karp, but a different, unknown number. I didn't know who it was, but my attention was piqued.

CHAPTER 2

"Who's this?" I asked after reading his message, knowing that there was no point in texting him.

"Someone you should know," he responded and I had the worst case of blue bean of my life, something I never even thought possible. I stood up right away on the bed, checking out the window by the bed. The room was small. It was tiny, but it was also a little homey, especially when I was texting my internet-only boyfriend.

"And who is that?" I asked, checking out the street. I couldn't see anyone over there, but that still didn't mean anything. It could be that he was elsewhere, probably watching me from afar with binoculars. It wouldn't be the first time that happened, so I was already alert to it.

My heart was tight and beating fast.

It was one thing chatting with someone I only knew on the internet, but another when someone else was calling me when I didn't even know his number.

"I'm going to be upfront about my name. It's Zakhar, and you are dealing with someone dangerous. You don't know how dangerous he is, and you should. This whole time, you were chatting with him and you didn't even know anything about him. I'm not your parent, but I would be pretty disappointed if I were."

I narrowed my eyes, my nostrils flaring. It was one thing him telling me that something was wrong with Karp and another him telling me that he was dangerous and that I shouldn't have anything to do with him.

"I don't know who you think you are, but you're not going to fool me."

"Really? It was so easy for him to fool you."

"If you think that you know so much about him, then you should tell me at least what his name is."

He chuckled and I could hear his footsteps from the other side of the call. I didn't know where he was, but it was pretty obvious that he was in an enclosed space, probably his room. This part of the city was littered with creeps, so he was probably just one more of them.

"It's Karp. You don't know me, but I know that he's been stalking you. He's been following you pretty closely these last months."

"If that's the case, then what is his end plan?" I asked, my heart was speeding up again. It was like I was going to have a heart attack and I was hoping that wasn't the case. I probably wouldn't survive it.

"That's something I'm trying to figure out myself," he responded and then breathed. I could tell that he wasn't American. Probably Russian as well, and that was the most likely possibility. Why? It was pretty simple. His voice was similar to Karp's, almost like they were twins.

"Just spit it out already and stop fucking with me," I demanded, showing my frustration in the tone of my voice. I was hoping that it was going to change his mind about what he was doing, but it was also possible he wasn't going to even be phased by it.

He breathed out loudly, saying, "I think I'm going to do something crazy."

"Well, I hope you aren't thinking about killing me or doing anything of the sort," I said, chuckling nervously. I had no idea why I was even kidding about something like that. I had no idea who that person was, and he could be from one of those Russian gangs. Wagner Group, was it? I was pretty sure that they were one of those, but I didn't even want to think about them right now.

Why? It was pretty simple. If I was one of their targets, I would probably not survive it for very long.

I was just walking out of the room when I heard heavy knocks on the door. Even though he didn't tell me anything about it – not yet - something about it was telling me that it was him, and that was making my heart feel tighter than before.

"Open up," he ordered and I rushed over to the door right away. It was like I was in a dream, but everything around me was still real. I could feel the coldness of the doorknob when I put my fingers around it and then, when I peered through the spy hole, I noticed that someone was indeed on the other side of the door.

He was tall. I had to be on my toes to see through the spy hole, but he didn't have to be. Or wouldn't, if he was right here with me in my room, and even though I knew I shouldn't, I was already imagining him entering my apartment room, standing right in front of me, and then doing… I had no idea what he would be doing, but it would probably be more than talking, something I was already getting used to.

"Are you going to open it or not?" He asked, his eyes glaring at me through the spy hole. I knew he wasn't seeing me, but he could feel me, which was something that was almost as threatening.

My hand was still on the doorknob and I knew I would be making a mistake if I locked the door. I was so nervous I didn't even realize I didn't unlock the door. Not yet, anyway. It was time to do something about that, and also to probably call the police.

Should I? I asked myself, but the question was more difficult than I thought possible to answer.

"I'm getting impatient here already," he grumbled and when I saw that he was going to start rapping on the door, I decided to do something about it before it was too late.

I opened the door right away and then I checked him out from bottom to top, and something came over me. I almost acted on it, but I was happy I didn't. I was almost going to throw myself into his arms, something that would show him I was already all wet for him, which I was.

"About damn time," he hissed, and then he rushed into the room, checking out what was behind him for a couple of seconds.

He was probably making sure that nobody was following him, and much less that Karp was aware that he was here.

And thinking about him, I was already wondering where he went. I just checked my phone and he didn't send me any new messages, my mind panicking, thinking that he was probably going to come back begging for my forgiveness. Even though he tried to come off tougher than he was, he was always so lonely that it was funny. But only sometimes, and only when I was drunk, which wasn't the case at the moment.

"Who the hell are you?" I asked, shutting the door with a loud thump. I locked it to make sure that nobody was coming in, but I was already thinking that it might be a mistake. Here I was with a stranger in my living room and he was towering in front of me, looking menacing and frightening.

I knew I couldn't and shouldn't even be thinking about it, but I was wondering if this was some kind of joke, where he was going to tell me that he was Karp all along and was using some kind of voice synthesizer to hide his true identity, but that didn't appear to be the case.

So much so that he was already ignoring me and then rushing over to the window. He peered outside, checking out the street. I went over to him and then I stopped behind him, wondering what was even going on in his mind.

"What are you doing?" I asked. Even though I probably shouldn't piss him off, it wasn't like I couldn't. After all, he was a stranger, was in my apartment, and he was - and I shouldn't even think of this as well – hot as hell.

He was well-built, tall, his muscles straining and showing even under his clothes, something that wasn't possible, especially when it came to weaker, punier men that didn't hold a candle to him.

I was probably making a mistake, but I felt good doing it.

CHAPTER 3

I tapped with my finger on his shoulder, calling his attention. He turned around quickly and then his eyes met mine. He knew that I wasn't here to play with him, thus it wasn't surprising when his eyes narrowed slightly. He was finally getting serious, something I was loving to see.

"What is it, *Torielle*?" He hissed and I liked that he knew my name. Even though he shouldn't, he still knew it. He was overly imposing in front of me and that was making my nipples hard, and they were like big pebbles right now. I could just imagine his fingers twitching and twirling them, and then he would put his tongue out and flick it over them, building up my climax.

I could just imagine it showering over me, making my body convulse. Was he thinking the same thing? I didn't know, but something about him was telling me that he probably was.

"Given that you are in my apartment, then you should at least pay your tax," I demanded, putting my hands on my waist. I was trying to look more determined and frightening than I was, but I knew it wasn't going to work. The reason was that he was already smiling, showing off how devilish he was.

"You really want me to do that?" He asked, putting his hand on my shoulder and then turning me around, pressing me against the wall. I wondered what he was going to do until I felt his fingers undoing the front of my shirt and then he pulled it to the sides, revealing my bust. He was ogling it and even though he didn't and wasn't saying anything about it, the fact that his lips were looking dry was telling me everything I needed to know.

"Yes," I responded and then I felt his fingers gliding over the front of my neck. They were calloused, just as I presumed they were. His hand was enormous and menacing, frightening even, and yet I didn't even think about begging for him to stop this.

My pussy was soaking wet and I was begging for him to start playing with it, something I knew he was already getting obsessed over.

"Fuck, you are so appetizing," he growled, his fingers undoing the zipper of my pants and then he lowered them, exposing my pair of panties.

I was aware that I was having sex with a stranger, but I didn't even consider stopping it. I was finally growing a backbone and having sex with a Russian. The only problem was that it wasn't happening with Karp, and yet... that was okay.

He got on his knees and then sniffed my pussy, loving it. His hands massaging my legs, he then looked up, finding my eyes. He licked his lips and then murmured, "I'm going to do so much with you that you are going to regret it."

I smiled, looking up and finding the ceiling. I knew I shouldn't say it, but I still did, "Then, you don't know anything about me."

He chuckled. I could feel his fingers pressing against my skin and it was sending all the right signals in my body. I knew that he wasn't a monster, but he could smell the scent coming out of my pussy, and it was making his dick rage and look so hard that it was poking against his pants.

I didn't even have to look down to see how massive and thick it was. I just knew.

He started to kiss my legs, moving his way down. He lowered my pants and then my pair of panties, and I stepped out of them a moment later. Zakhar was careful while doing that, taking his time. Funny thing this was. I knew I would eventually find myself in this kind of situation, but I thought it was going to happen with Karp and not with a stranger that said he knew who he was.

His fingers played with my toes before he pulled my pants and panties up. He tossed them behind him and then kissed my legs some more, moving down to my toes. His fingers played with them, brushing them between the gaps, and then he looked up.

He didn't lock his eyes with me, opting to make his way back up instead. He moved his body up and when his face was right in front of my cunt, he breathed my scent slowly. He did that so slowly that it was intoxicating and tormenting.

I could feel my body getting so hot it was inconceivable to think that it was different moments before. He took another deep breath and then inched his hand to my pussy. Noticing that I was growing uncomfortable, given that I was still standing and he was on his knees, he moved me to the couch, making me perch on its right arm with my legs wide open.

"Fuck, Torielle, you are so delicious," he purred and even though it was a little corny, I didn't mind it. In fact, I welcomed it. I felt his fingers brushing against my pussy folds, playing with them, moving them, and applying pressure when necessary.

He was so experienced. He knew how and when to press all the right buttons.

Zakhar even started to scratch and rub at my clit, making my body tremble. My knees were weak, but it didn't matter. I was seated on the couch and his hands were gripping my knees, making it impossible for me to fall anywhere, which was relieving. I wasn't going to do anything that could piss him off.

Even breathing was becoming more difficult, but I was welcoming it. His fingers were all over my flower and then, when he was growing tired of that, he dug one of them inside my cunt, rubbing it in there. Each swirl and thrust of his finger sent shockwaves of pleasure in my body, showing me that I had to do something to match his rhythm. It was for that reason that I started to rub and play with my nipples after finally getting rid of my bra. I'd feared that it would take me a lot more time until we reached that level, but we didn't. And I was surprised by that.

He stopped all of a sudden, making me reopen my eyes and then glance down. I wondered what he was thinking, but then he decided to answer that even though I didn't even say anything yet.

"I'm just making sure that you are breathing, or at least that you have some time to breathe," he responded and then I chuckled.

"Really? I didn't think you were so caring when it came to me. I mean, I don't even know you," I said and he smirked.

"There's something else I want to do with you," Zakhar announced and when I was going to ask him what that was, he slid his tongue out of his mouth. So, it was that thing. My heart was already speeding up, my mind loving what was about to happen.

He started to lick my pussy slowly at the beginning. And even when I figured he was going to start picking up the pace, he didn't. His licks were long, controlled, measured, and he knew what he was doing. And one more thing Zakhar knew he was doing? He was savoring my orgasm. He was coating his tongue with it and was loving it.

My body could almost not contain it any longer, my incoming and impending climax growing with each passing second. I knew that when it hit me, it would hit me so hard that I would start to convulse. My body was starting to tremble and I would come all over his face, something I was sure he was looking forward to.

"Give me everything you have. I crave your cunt juices so badly," he purred and his face, his tongue, his lips, and even his cheeks were all smeared with my release, something that he was loving. I could tell that from the way he was smiling.

"I think that much more than that is going to come out," I announced as my fingers didn't stop dancing over my nipples, rubbing, twirling them, massaging and palming my boobs in their free time. Given the smile on his face, I could tell that he was enjoying what he was seeing.

So much so that it wasn't surprising when he neared his face to my cunt, flicking his tongue against it a couple of times. When he felt that he brought me over the edge, he stretched his smile. He knew that it was happening and that he was going to reap the benefits.

It was for that reason that he was also already widening his mouth and then, when my body started to convulse and I was coming all over his face, he was licking it all up with lust in his eyes.

It was the most amazing, uncontrollable climax of my life.

CHAPTER 4

nd it didn't stop there. Zakhar even licked the side of his lips, making sure that he was getting everything. He flicked his tongue one last time and then put it back inside his mouth. I was a little disappointed, seeing that. Zakhar must have noticed the disappointment in my face, for he immediately said, "Don't worry, it doesn't stop here."

I knew he was planning on doing things even worse to me, but I didn't think that he wasn't going to have time.

And I knew he wasn't lying when he said that, but then we heard knocks on the door. Our heads snapped to it and we both didn't know what to do, except for the fact that something needed to be done. I heard him gulping and I knew that couldn't mean anything good, something that was already making my mind feel troubled.

"I should go to the door," I said, aware of the fact that I was fully naked. I didn't even have my bra on, just as it was supposed to be, especially when I had a tall and imposing Russian in my living room. He also stood up slowly and was still where I left him, doing nothing in particular.

"I'm going to be here, watching over you just in case," he promised as his dick begged to come out of his pants. And one more thing that was also playing a role in this situation? It was the fact that I wanted to see his cock out of his pants as well.

It was a pity that, until then, we had to deal with whoever was on the other side of the door and still rapping on it.

I didn't say anything, going on my toes to look through the spy hole. I feared I was going to find a killer about to shoot me through the door. After all, it was thick and heavy, but it would do nothing against a bullet.

And I knew I didn't have reasons to fear for my life, but I still was. That was just how it was with me.

I wrapped my fingers around the doorknob when I peered in the spy hole. For a moment, I couldn't make out what my eyes were seeing. The man that was on the other side was tall, imposing, and overall wide. He was more massive than anyone I had seen before in my life, including Zakhar. Given that he was just behind me and was also still hard, I wasn't going to say anything about that. I wasn't crazy, after all.

I knew what guys of his type were like. They were always jealous and obsessed with women like me.

"Open up, Torielle," the man ordered, and I knew his voice. It was the same voice on the phone, which meant that he could only be Karp, and that was something I wasn't expecting. It caught me off guard and I almost lost my balance, but only for a short while. I recovered it right away and hoped that Zakhar didn't notice it. After all, I didn't want him to get worried about me. "I know you are in there."

I cleared my throat. Karp was here and Zakhar said that he was a killer, who probably came here to murder me and him. I couldn't take the chance, and I wasn't going to. Even though he was a cool guy when we were talking over the phone, I knew I was smarter than most people thought I was, including him.

I stepped away from the door when I heard him kicking it with all of his strength, then the hinges broke, and the door fell with a heavy thud on the floor. I was happy that I was far away from it so that it didn't even come close to hitting me, but this was still frightening. My mouth almost let out a little scream. It only didn't because I covered it with my hand.

"What's the meaning of this?" Zakhar growled, marching to stand behind me. Even though this place was dangerous and the situation that was developing before my eyes was equally so, I felt safe knowing that he was behind me. His hand was on my waist and he was pulling me closer to him, something that showed how much he cared.

"It's you, isn't it?" Karp asked, drawing his gun out and then pointing it at Zakhar, and even at me. I let out a scream this time, and nothing could have been done to prevent it. I felt a little ashamed of it. I always thought I was much more courageous than I was showing right now.

His eyes checked me out from bottom to top, smiling. What a bastard. He was finding it funny that I was naked. Not to mention that the door was knocked off the hinges and was on the floor. Anyone walking down the hallway could see me naked and I wouldn't be able to do anything about it, something that was frightening and also arousing me. It was weird. Not even I could describe what was going on with me.

"It's me, yeah, buddy," Zakhar replied and I noticed that they were both still speaking English, even though they didn't have to. They respected me, even though I was in a position where I shouldn't be getting so much respect. After all, I was naked, Zakhar had his arm around me and Karp had his gun pointed at me, even though he was trying to aim it at Zakhar. He was his enemy and not me, of course.

"What are you going to do?" I asked, breaking free from Zakhar's arm and then finding myself standing between the two of them. The door not giving us privacy was annoying, but it wasn't like there was anything I could do about it. I was going to have to pretend that nobody could just walk into the room and find themselves in this hairy situation.

"I'm going to kill him," Zakhar growled, also drawing out his gun. He only didn't fire it because I was standing between him and his nemesis. Now that I was noticing it, they were very much alike. Not only were they Russians, but they were also white, had short blond hair, harsh facial features, and their lips were tight and small, with some beard on their faces still to be made.

Even the smell of their perfumes was the same. I never thought that I was going to find two men that were so similar. It was almost like they were twins.

"No, you aren't going to do anything. I don't want to see bloodshed in my apartment," I stated and then he lowered his gun, something I thought wasn't going to happen – at least, not so easily.

"What do you mean?" Zakhar asked and he had not lowered his gun yet. Seeing that, I decided to do something that wasn't common for me. I put my hand on the barrel of his gun and then I forced him to lower it. He did, his eyes finding mine.

Whatever we had going on before, our sexy time, was long gone, and I had no idea if it was going to be possible to recover it.

"We need to make a compromise," I proposed.

"What kind of compromise?" Zakhar asked. Even though he didn't lift his gun back up, he still had it in his hand, and that was something I was going to fix soon enough.

"I know what's going on in your mind. You both want me, right?" I asked and they both gulped. I knew I was going to impress them, but I didn't think it was going to be so easy. And I didn't think that it was going to make them almost drop their guns, too.

"It's true. We both want you," they said at the same time and it was the confirmation I was looking for. They both wanted me and we could do something so that they didn't have to kill each other.

"Well, in that case, then you can both have me. Are you okay with that?"

They glanced at each other and then when I was already getting a little annoyed that they were taking too long to respond, they finally did, "I think that we can make it happen, yeah."

"Perfect." Even though I was trying to show that I wasn't concerned and utterly frightened, I still let out a sigh of relief. "Then we can start doing what we should be doing."

My lips were dry. I was going to do this even though we couldn't put the door back in place and it was going to be mad and wild, but still very much rewarding.

CHAPTER 5

Sashaying over to Karp, I locked my eyes with his. It was a long, solitary moment between the two of us. Even though he was probably from the Wagner Group, a man willing to kill anyone for money, and almost a head taller than me, he was falling under my spell.

"I'm sure you are a big guy and I want to find out just how big," I teased and my voice was throaty and low. I didn't waste any time, dropping to my knees right away. My face was right in front of his crotch and I could already smell the musky scent that was coming out of it. And something stronger than that was the woody smell of his perfume, and it was excellent. It was hitting all the right buttons in me and hardening my nipples even harder than they were.

His eyes couldn't stop moving up and down and left and right, checking me out. His lips were dry. I could tell that thanks to the skin flakes on them. Then, he gulped again. He was so aroused that his dick was poking against his pants, inviting me to lower them.

And it was then I knew that only one thing could be done right now.

I pinched his zipper, lowering it. It happened slowly, but it was rewarding. When the front of his pants was open, I could finally see a glimpse of his bulge. It was already big, and it could grow even bigger. Not to mention that I couldn't even see all of it, something that was making me salivate.

"Hurry up. I don't have all the time in the world," Zakhar hissed, annoying me, but I was going to forgive him for that. After all, this was our first time together and there were still so many things to learn about each other.

I put my fingers under the bands of his pants and then I lowered them, finally revealing the full extent of his bulge. It was bigger and plumper than I thought possible. My nipples were dry and my heart was speeding up. I was growing anxious and there was nothing I could do about it.

I started to palm and massage his bulge, loving it. I could feel his dick hardening, and there was only one thing I could do about it. It was for that reason that I snuck my fingers under his pair of briefs as well, lowering it. I saw the head of his prick slipping out and then the rest of it, gracing me with its presence.

I licked my lips. I didn't think there was a cock better than this one, even though I was aware that I still hadn't seen Zakhar's. That was something I was going to fix soon enough, though.

It was pointing at me and it was raging and incredibly hard. He was almost throbbing and erupting. In the meantime, I was barely aware of the fact that someone had just walked down the hallway, stopped to check out what was happening in my living room, and then they hurried off as quickly as they could. I didn't even have time to find out the gender of that person.

It wasn't like it mattered, anyway.

I checked out his balls, noticing how low they hung. I moved my hand down and then I cupped them, or tried to. They were bigger and heavier than I thought, and I could only imagine how much milk he had in them. I could only imagine what it was going to be like when he was coming inside of me, filling me with his seed.

I heard someone stopping behind me and that could only be Zakhar. I heard him undoing his zipper and then his pants fell down, revealing his prick. I had to turn around quickly and then I found his rod right in front of my face, where my mouth was. It was the perfect height for a blowjob, something I knew he was looking forward to.

"Torielle, you have a choice you need to make. You can suck him off first or you can do that for me before."

I looked up, finding his eyes.

"I don't know if I can make that choice. I don't want to have favorites," I announced, my voice so low it was almost impossible for me to hear it. And if that was the case, I wondered if he even made out what I said.

But then, he replied by rubbing the palm of his hand on my forehead.

"Don't worry, princess. We don't want you to have favorites."

The way he was saying that was almost like they were going to invite more of their friends over, which was something I could look forward to, especially if I knew it could happen. But it wasn't like I was even going to ask them that question, so I just put it where it wasn't going to bother me.

I shut my eyes and I made a choice. Karp was the first one that showed up in my life, thus I owed him something, and that something should be this amazing blowjob I was going to give him.

I studied his prick one more time, checking out the slit, his balls, the fact that he'd shaved, the slight throbbing of his manhood, and also the fact that he really was probably 10 inches long, something that wasn't possible for someone who didn't have the same pedigree.

Without saying anything else and hoping that I wasn't going to disappoint Zakhar, I wrapped my fingers around Karp's slab of meat. I felt his legs weakening when I did that and then he took a step toward me, his cockhead brushing against my lips.

I saw him doing that, but it was still a surprise when it did.

I also felt how good the saltiness of his pre-come on my lips was, and I had to put my tongue out and lick it. I smiled devilishly, looking up. He was looking down at me and I could see how devilish his thoughts were. He was going to knock me up, take my virginity, and I was welcoming those things.

I started to stroke his manhood slowly, my hand moving up and down. It took about five seconds to cover the entire path, and I continued to do that slowly. In the meantime, Zakhar was also jacking off slowly behind me. I had no idea if he was going to blow his load all over my backside, but I was hoping he wasn't going to do that. When he came, I was hoping that he was going to do so in my cunt.

"It should be prohibited, the way you are doing this so excruciatingly slow," he grumbled and I knew he had a point, but given that this was my first time sucking off a guy, I wanted to make it a memorable moment.

I closed my eyes after I got tired of stroking his massive, oversized dick. I lowered my head and then I enclosed my lips around his cockhead, brushing my tongue over and over on the underside of it. If his legs were already shaking before and looking weak, now they were even more so and I was worried that he was going to blow his load in my mouth. I mean, it wouldn't be all bad if it happened, but I was still hoping that things were going to follow the direction I wanted.

I wasn't even going to dare put more of his prick in my mouth than I already had. I didn't think it would fit, not to mention that I didn't want to start gagging, too.

I just focused on swirling my tongue around his cockhead and especially on the underside of it, where I knew he was even more sensitive. He put his hand on my head, probably to make sure I wasn't going to move it away anytime soon. Regardless, when I knew he was close to coming, I would certainly pull it back.

The saltiness of his pre-come was almost overwhelming me and I knew that when I was done, it would be hard for me to savor the taste of the food I was going to eat. I already had dinner tonight, but tomorrow morning I was going to have brunch and I had no idea if I was going to be hungry enough for it, especially if he unloaded his milk inside my mouth.

And when I felt that his cock was already throbbing more violently than it should, I pulled my head back. I feared that he was going to block it with his hand, but he didn't, which was relieving. I figured that he only did that because Zakhar was right behind him and he wanted me to do the same I did for him.

And I was going to. Turning around and finding his eyes and the way that he was stroking his big slab of meat, I knew he wanted me to suck him off right away.

CHAPTER 6

"Took your sweet time, didn't you, princess?" He asked, his tone showing that he didn't like it. And yet, he wasn't going to do anything about it. Why? It was pretty simple. He wanted me to start sucking him off right away and I was going to do just that. My eyes examined his prick and it was as massive as Karp's, but maybe also slightly bigger. It was difficult to be certain of that when I didn't have a ruler. It wasn't like that mattered anyway, though. My pussy was soaking wet, my mind dreaming about all the ways that they were going to hurt me when they were inside of me.

"Let's do something different this time," I proposed, standing up as I wrapped my fingers around his rod. I took him with me to the bed and then I lied down on it. I didn't have to tell him what I wanted to do and then he followed my lead, climbing with me.

Karp came over as well and the devilish smile on his face told me that he was jubilant about this as well.

"You are always so innovative, Torielle," he purred, climbing onto the bed so that he was the one closer to my pussy. I felt his hands sagging the bed and then him putting out his tongue, flicking it over my pussy. He took off his clothes and then I could finally see how perfect his body was, his muscles shining off the light coming from the bulb.

"I can do a lot more than this."

He widened his smile slightly. "Like what?" He asked, flicking his tongue over my pussy again. The way he was doing that was so lovely and arousing, my body shaking and beginning to show me that it was going to start convulsing if he didn't slow down.

"Like this," I replied, and then Zakhar was the one standing behind me and also above me, his body positioned in the other direction. I could feel his lips pressing against my neck, pecking it. Shifting again, he positioned his prick so that it was right in front of my lips and then he didn't waste any time before lowering his hips. His dick went right into my mouth and I welcomed it.

He only put the mushroom-shaped head inside, but it was enough for me. I started to swirl my tongue around it, focusing on the underside, just like I did for Karp. I could see his body shaking and I could feel his prick throbbing in my mouth, and it was delicious. He was already leaking his pre-come, and it was as salty as Karp's.

In the meantime, the latter was happy that he was the one all over my pussy. He gave it another long, powerful lick, looking up at me. Our eyes met and then he said, "I have something that is a suspicion of mine, but I know it's ridiculous. I don't think I should even say what it is."

"Well? Spit it out already. I'm not here to waste time," I chided him after Zakhar pulled his dong out of my mouth. He did that so that I could talk to Karp, something I was grateful for. He was mindful of my needs even when he didn't need to be. I thought he was going to be way more competitive with Karp for my attention.

And yet, he wanted his rod back inside my mouth right away, and I was going to do that, but only after I was done talking with his nemesis.

"You are a virgin, aren't you?" He asked, his fingers brushing against my pussy folds. Then, as if to tease me even more than I was, he started to rub my clit, and it was sending shockwaves of pleasure in my body. It was difficult to control it and if he kept on doing that, I was going to reach my climax.

I nodded and bit my bottom lip. Zakhar was still trying to insert his prick back into my mouth, but he couldn't, thanks to the way that I kept on opening and closing my lips as I talked.

But then, he stopped when he heard my answer. "Wait, you are a virgin?" He asked, but it wasn't really a question. It was more like he was surprised by my answer and needed to say something, regardless of what it was.

I nodded again, urging both of them to do their manly duty. They wanted to take my virginity and they were welcome to do that.

But after he better processed and understood what was going on, he widened his smile. "Well, we better do something about that, don't you think, buddy?" He asked his nemesis.

Karp nodded, pulled me up so that I was with my legs over his shoulders, and then he started to prod and play with my pussy, using his prick to do so.

He was taking his time and I knew that it wasn't going to take much longer. My body was suspended in the air and Zakhar wasn't going to take his time doing what he wanted. It was for that reason that he grabbed me by my shoulders and then lowered my head so that my lips were already brushing over his cockhead. I felt that familiar, inciting taste of his pre-come, and then I licked my lips.

I was going to be sucking him off while his friend finally took my virginity, and I was happy that he wasn't salty about that.

When he understood that he couldn't extend this any longer than it already was, he pried open my mouth with his fingers and then eased his prick in there, going all the way down my throat. "Sorry, princess, but I want it all inside your mouth this time."

I felt his cockhead scratching against the back of my throat and I started to gag. I hoped that he was going to slow down a little, but he didn't. He started to roll his hips and pound in and out of me, turning my throat and mouth into his playthings, abusing them without blowbacks from me.

"Fuck, your mouth is so tight and warm," he murmured as he continued on pounding in and out of me, making me feel everything I thought I was going to feel. My body was heating up and my heart was accelerating. I knew I wasn't going to last much longer, and I didn't.

My body started to convulse and it was the most thrilling, incredible thing that ever happened in my life. And I didn't even lose my virginity properly yet. I still had my hymen, but not for much longer, I could tell. Karp was already pressing against it and then, with a thrust of his hips, he popped it. It happened so quickly that it was almost like it didn't matter, but it did. I was finally going to be able to tell my bitch friends about what happened tonight.

"She's equally as tight down here," Karp murmured more to himself than to anyone. And seconds later, he didn't hold back as he started to ram his manhood in and out of me, going all the way to the end of my tunnel, and then rubbing against my G-spot with each thrust of his, making my body shake out of control.

And I was, pretty much. I was trapped between these two hunky beats and they were using that to their advantage.

It was for that reason that I wasn't surprised when they switched up, and now Zakhar was the one pounding in and out of me, his dick feeling so big. He was stretching my walls and even though it hurt a lot, I didn't say anything about it. The only thing I was doing with my mouth right now was sucking off Karp again, and I could tell that he could come one more time, something I was looking forward to.

And then, he did. His balls started to unload his come inside my mouth and it was as delicious and as salty as before. It was everywhere, sticky, warm, and thick. It was so viscous that it was going to take some time until it went down my throat, and even then I didn't say anything about it.

I was only a little sad when he finally pulled out

I wished he was going to stay in my mouth for all of eternity, but it was obvious he couldn't do that. So much so that he was already panting and his eyes were closing. He plopped down on my bed and fell asleep.

In the meantime, Zakhar was coming inside of me and I wasn't even thinking about doing anything to prevent pregnancy. I wanted to have their baby, even though I knew I wasn't going to know who the father was. It wasn't like that mattered much, anyway.

What mattered was being their woman, and I was making

that happen.

EPILOGUE

"**I** thought that it was going to work out between us," he said, and his name was Renell. He was someone that thought he was going to become my boyfriend, but it didn't happen that way. Why? It was pretty simple. I found someone that truly, utterly completed me, and he was none other than Karp. And also Zakhar. They were in Karp's car, waiting for me. The drumming of their fingers on the console and the steering wheel of the car told me everything I needed to know. They were already impatient that I was taking so long to go back there.

If only it was so easy, especially for someone like me that didn't like breaking hearts. That was why I was waiting so long. I wanted to make sure that Renell truly lost me and that he could do nothing about it.

I shifted my weight, saying, "It was never going to work. You were illusioned by the possibility of it working, but it was never going to. I told you that I was even looking for someone else, and I found that. Two of them, actually, to be honest."

He peered over my shoulder, finding the guys in the car. Even though he didn't know anything about them, he knew better than to make questions that shouldn't be answered.

And yet, I felt like Renell was about to do something stupid right now.

It was for that reason I was already throwing myself to the side and putting myself in front of him. I didn't want to see bloodshed, especially if it happened because of me. I put my hands on his chest and shoved him backward slightly. He took a step back, his eyes narrowing.

"I don't know who they are, but I still want to talk to them. I want to make sure that you are going to be okay no matter what happens."

I shook my head. "That's not going to happen. I don't think it's something you should do or that it's a good idea."

He tried to push me aside, but I was stronger than that. I wasn't someone he could just push aside easily, and he was frustrated by that. So much so that he huffed slightly.

"I can't believe you are doing something like this to me," he said and I could almost see a tear coming out of his eye. But he was also stronger than that and pushed his tear back. It wasn't visible anymore, which was something I was grateful for. If there was something I also didn't like at all, it was seeing a man crying.

"It's my decision and you can't change it."

"Obviously," he hissed before slamming the door shut in my face, and then I heard him retreating, leaving me with nothing else to say. I turned around and rested my back on the wall of his house, letting my butt fall to the floor alongside the rest of my body. I looked up and I found the moon. It was pretty and was glowing with the stars, making the night feel inviting, but it was also much more than that.

It wasn't like I had much time to think about that as well, I thought.

Just as I closed my eyes and lowered my head, I heard footsteps approaching me. When I reopened my eyes, I found none other than Karp and Zakhar coming over to me. I knew it was them, so it wasn't a surprise. I was just hoping that I was going to have some more privacy so that I could think about everything that happened. It wasn't a true break up, but it still hurt me.

"You are stronger than this, princess," Karp said and it was true. So much so that I only needed to hear his words to stand back up. He offered me his hand, which I took. I felt it tugging me back up and then, in less than a second, I was back on my feet.

His hands gripped my shoulders and he kept me in place. His eyes met mine and, for a moment, I couldn't think about anything.

It was like time was frozen and he was telling me so many things. And yet, there was no point in thinking about them right now. Anything we wanted to do, we could always do it at any time.

He let go of my shoulders and then wrapped his arm over them, taking me back to their car. He opened the door for me and I sat down heavily. I let out a sigh of relief as I remembered that the worst was over. I was in such a bad moment in my life before this, thinking that everything was going wrong for me. I always thought I wasn't going to find someone who I wanted to be with.

And when I feared that things were already ending for tonight, Zakhar, who was sitting behind me, snuck his fingers under my shirt and pulled it up and then over my head. His hands didn't waste time, in a moment going for my breasts. He started to massage them, his fingers knowing where to apply pressure.

I didn't think it was possible, but it looked like they were going to do it right here, right in front of my 'ex-boyfriend's' house, and it was going to be as exciting as it was going to be wrong. After all, my pussy was already soaking wet and I could already wonder about all the dirty, nasty little things that we were going to do together.

Just moaning and groaning as loudly as I could wasn't going to be sufficient.

The End

You can find the first three books here:

1. Dirty Doctors
2. Dirty Bikers
3. Dirty Cowboys

Or you can also read a sneak peek for book 1 on the next page. Lastly, leave your review. Your feedback helps me improve.

TEASER: DIRTY DOCTORS

Series: Plus Size - 1

I wiped the sweat off my forehead, thinking that things couldn't be getting any worse for me even if I tried to. I was in front of the car and then I popped up the engine's lid, coughing when smoke hit my face. It smelled pretty bad and it was dark, reminding me that whatever was going on here, it wasn't good for me, especially given that I wanted to get to the airport as soon as possible. I had a trip planned to go to Italy, where I was going to spend my well-earned vacation.

It was dark and the moon was high in the sky. It was a full moon, which was extremely bright. My eyes couldn't spot many clouds in the sky, something that I didn't think much of. The stars twinkled in the deadness of the night, making me feel that they were pretty much part of the only thing keeping me company here.

My car wasn't old, but it wasn't a top model either. So much so that it wasn't surprising that it broke down on me right when I was still traveling in and crossing the countryside.

Where I was, I couldn't even see the nearest city, which was saying something. The state where I was didn't have much in terms of the countryside. Some farms populated the region, but they weren't part of the dominating presence. That was, of course, the cities and the villages.

I shook my head and started to go to the right of the car when my eyes spotted two glowing orbs in the distance. For a moment, I didn't think much of them, overlooking them when the following thought crossed my mind - even though I was pretty much alone here and didn't think that anyone was going to come this way, it was possible I got lucky this time.

I waved my arms over my head, hoping that they were going to notice that I was stranded on the road. It was a dirt road, so it wasn't surprising when they shot past me in their car that dust and dirt were kicked up by their tires, making me cough again.

I waved my hands in front of my face, stepping away from the smoke of those things that they must have generated on purpose. I thought for a moment that they weren't going to stop, but a smile crept up on my face when I noticed that I was wrong.

The red lights of their car grew in intensity as they pulled back, stopping by my side. I peered inside the vehicle as I noticed that it really was two men driving their Mustang. I didn't think much of it, but soon I realized that they were hot and burly.

I took a second to dissect them with my eyes. My eyes went up and down slowly, carefully analyzing who they appeared to be. I was just a little paranoid that they were criminals. Given the high-class look on their faces, I didn't think that they were, but I couldn't be sure, either.

What I was sure about was that they were my type. So much so that my nipples were getting slightly hard, which was something that didn't happen often anymore these days. One of the reasons for that was that after realizing that my crush didn't want anything to do with me, I lost any and all interest I had in love. It faded out of my mind and I didn't think it would ever come back.

They didn't have much in terms of clothes, opting for plain shirts, jean shorts, dark shoes, and not much more than that. I noticed that one of the guys had short, dark hair and that the other had slightly longer hair, but that it was blond.

They both had some scruff on their faces, suggesting that they hadn't shaved in a while. I wondered if that meant they had been on the road for some time already, but I didn't think that it was prudent of me to ask them about that.

I decided not to. After all, my mind was more preoccupied with other things.

The one that was sitting closest to me analyzed me with his eyes, smiling softly. I had no idea what that meant, but I was beginning to grow a little more suspicious of what it could be.

I didn't want to think that he harbored dirty, secret thoughts regarding me, but that appeared to be the case.

I could see the glint of the color of his eyes. They were the same color as jade, which was so pretty that it made me want to do things with him that, otherwise, I wouldn't even be thinking about right now.

It wasn't just that my nipples were hard right now, but that they were like little pebbles on my breasts.

"Need a little help with something, miss?" He asked, opening the door of his car and then stepping out alongside his friend. When they shut the door of their cars, I noticed how tall they were. They were much taller than me, which was one other thing that made them the eye candies they were.

They tipped up their chins, looking more confident. I certainly didn't think that I was going to find myself in the presence of such burly, confident men, but here I was. They were so imposing that they made me feel smaller than I was, which wasn't something that happened often.

After all, I was a plus-size girl with plenty of curves. Perhaps that was something that they found attractive about me, which was a possibility. The way that their eyes were scanning me told me that, too. I stepped away from them, but then my butt touched the frame of the car. I knew that I had nowhere to escape to, not that I was thinking about doing that, though...

MORE BOOKS LIKE THIS ONE

SERIES - FIRST TIME QUICKIES

They compete over her, want every part of her, and nothing can stop them.

1. Claiming her Age Gap: Reverse Harem Mafia

2. Selling her Age Gap: Reverse Harem Mafia

3. Loving her Age Gap: Reverse Harem Mafia

Or download all the books in this convenient, cheap bundle:

1. Our Princess: Mafia Reverse Harem Bundle

SERIES - IN PUBLIC

It's all about doing it in public, shamelessly, and dominating their exposed princesses.

1. Fed from Behind: Rear Entrance Devoured by Multiple Men

2. Fed from Behind: Tight Squeeze by Multiple Men

3. Fed from Behind: Taken by Multiple Men on Christmas Day

4. Fed from Behind: Tight Squeeze in front of the Christmas Tree

5. Tight Squeeze: Petite for Big Alpha Men of the House

ABOUT THE AUTHOR

Leandra Camilli's obsession? Writing dirty, steamy stories that make her readers drool. She loves her Alpha males, hucows, sissies, and futas. If you're searching for those kinds of books, look no further.

With a cup of coffee on her table and warm socks on, she writes almost every day. Leandra Camilli has featured in several top 100 categories in the store, and she publishes weekly.